For Lincoln
(Who is no monster at all!)
—R. S.

For Alek and Kyle
—D. S.

MARGARET K. McELDERRY BOOKS
An imprint of Simon & Schuster Children's Publishing Division
1230 Avenue of the Americas, New York, New York 10020
Text copyright © 2017 by Rob Sanders
Illustrations copyright © 2017 by Dan Santat
All rights reserved, including the right of reproduction
in whole or in part in any form.
MARGARET K. McELDERRY BOOKS is a trademark of Simon & Schuster, Inc.
For information about special discounts for bulk purchases,
please contact Simon & Schuster Special Sales at 1-866-506-1949
or business@simonandschuster.com.
The Simon & Schuster Speakers Bureau can bring authors to your live event.
For more information or to book an event, contact the Simon & Schuster
Speakers Bureau at 1-866-248-3049 or visit our website
at www.simonspeakers.com.
Book design by Lauren Rille
The text for this book was set in Zalderdash.
The illustrations for this book were rendered in watercolor, pencil,
and Photoshop.
Manufactured in China
0217 SCP
First Edition
10 9 8 7 6 5 4 3 2 1
Library of Congress Cataloging-in-Publication Data
Names: Sanders, Rob, 1958– author. | Santat, Dan, illustrator.
Title: Rodzilla / Rob Sanders ; Illustrated by Dan Santat.
Description: First edition. | New York : Margaret K. McElderry Books, [2017] |
Summary: "A toddler causes Godzilla-like mayhem in the city of his playpen"—
Provided by publisher.
Identifiers: LCCN 2016022301 (print) | LCCN 2016042672 (eBook) |
ISBN 9781481457798 (hardcover) | ISBN 9781481457804 (eBook)
Subjects: | CYAC: Play—Fiction. | Imagination—Fiction.
Classification: LCC PZ7.S19785 Rod 2017 (print) | LCC PZ7.S19785 (eBook) |
DDC [E]—dc23
LC record available at https://lccn.loc.gov/2016022301

WELCOME TO
MEGALOPOLIS

RODZILLA

written by
Rob Sanders

illustrated by
Dan Santat

Margaret K. McElderry Books • New York London Toronto Sydney New Delhi

Big, bad trouble
in Megalopolis.
This is Channel 15
News reporting, and . . .
one moment, please . . .

WOBBLE-
WOBBLE-
WOBBLE.
TODDLE-CLUNK.

Oh no!
A soft, squishy monster
has escaped into the city!

He's huge.
He's pudgy.
He's . . .

Pvvvt!
What's that smell?

Rodzilla is shooting . . .
stink-rays!

Ack! Only a mother
could love such a creature.

Look out! . . . He's . . . heading . . . to . . .
City Center Park!

Rodzilla has unleashed . . .

a slime missile!
Drivers are losing control of their vehicles.

Pedestrians must duck for cover.

This just in: Rodzilla has stopped.
He's grabbing his tummy, and . . .

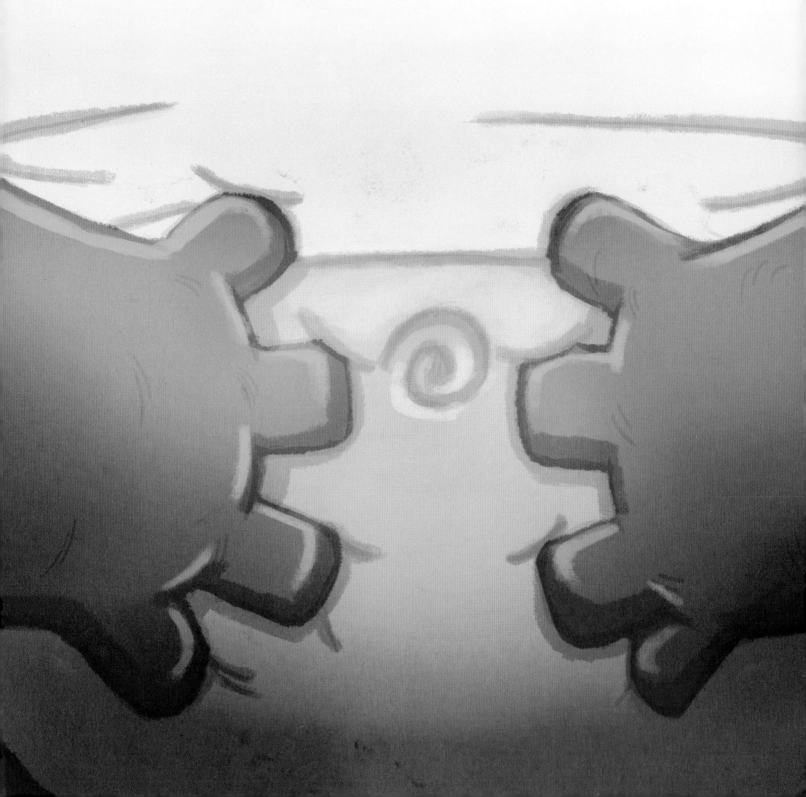

SPLOSH!
SPLASH!
SQUISH!

BLECK!

He's hurled an attack!
Rodzilla has hurled
an attack!

Firefighters are hosing him down.
Police are trying to herd him out of the city.

Wait! Rodzilla is wobbling. He's tottering.
He's about to . . .

Could this be the end of Rodzilla?

Rodzilla cannot be stopped.
And now . . . he's . . . heading . . . downtown!

Rodzilla has grabbed a taxi . . . *and* a bus.

He's the mightiest creature to ever roam the streets.
Residents can only stare at this chubby monstrosity.
They gaze in horror at his toothless grin.

This just in:
Rodzilla has reached Skyscraper Tower.
He is now—oh, my word—
Rodzilla is now
CLIMBING UP THE BUILDING!

Workers are racing away in fear.

I'm standing with several eyewitnesses, waiting for . . .

It's an earsplitting cry.
Rodzilla's sobs echo through the streets.
His tears are raining down.
A flood warning has just been released!

What's that?

I've just gotten word that two brave citizens are on the elevator heading up to Rodzilla.

The elevator doors jerk open.

They've come face-to-face
with the creature.
Rodzilla has taken one step . . .

and another . . .

and another. . . .

"Oh, Rodney!" Mommy exclaims.
"You're such a little monster," says Daddy.

Rodzilla has been captured!
I repeat, Rodzilla has been captured!

The city is safe at last.
Megalopians can breathe a sigh of relief.

Or can they?